The Greatest Mother's Day of All

Anne Mangan

Illustrated by Tamsin Ainslie

Angus&Robertson
An imprint of HarperCollinsChildrn'sBook

Angus&Robertson
An imprint of HarperCollins*Publishers*, Australia

First published in Australia in 2012
by HarperCollins*Publishers* Australia Pty Limited
ABN 36 009 913 517
harpercollins.com.au

Text copyright © Anne Mangan 2012
Illustrations copyright © Tamsin Ainslie 2012

HarperCollins*Publishers*
Level 13, 201 Elizabeth Street, Sydney NSW 2000, Australia
31 View Road, Glenfield, Auckland 0627, New Zealand
A 53, Sector 57, Noida, UP, India
1 London Bridge Street, London SE1 9GF, United Kingdom
2 Bloor Street East, 20th floor, Toronto, Ontario M4W 1A8, Canada
195 Broadway, New York, NY 10007, USA

National Library of Australia Cataloguing-in-Publication entry

Mangan, Anne.The greatest Mother's Day of all / written by Anne Mangan;
illustrated by Tamsin Ainslie.
9780732293345 (hbk.)
For primary school age.
Mothers--Juvenile fiction.
Mother and child--Juvenile fiction.
Other Authors/Contributors:
Ainslie, Tamsin, 1974-
A823.3

Tamsin Ainslie used pencil and gouache on watercolour paper to produce the artwork for this book.
Cover design and internal design by Matt Stanton, HarperCollins Design Studio
Typeset in Cambridge Serial
Colour reproduction by Graphic Print Group, Adelaide, South Australia
Printed by RR Donnelley in China, on 128gsm Matt Art

5 4 3 2   16 17 18 19

To all mothers,
in particular my mum Gertie,
for being the greatest mother of all.

A.M.

To Sue Reynolds for making so many
Mother's Days the greatest of all.

T.A.

With Mother's Day a day away,
the shops were full of noise.
Frazzled dads were pleading with kids,
'Stop playing with the toys!'

Dad was running out of time
to buy Mum something smelly.
He really had to get back home
… for the football on the telly.

A litre bottle of perfume?
Scented candle or soap in a jar?
Dad quickly grabbed one of each
and piled the kids back in the car.

At home they wrapped the presents,
leaving a mess upon the floor.
The kids told Mum they could not
tell her who the gifts were for.

Dad woke the kids next morning,
to make Mum breakfast in bed.
He was not too sure where things were kept,
so the kids took charge instead.

They made lumpy pancakes and burnt the toast,
dirty dishes were everywhere.

The children looked like quite a sight
with egg and flour in their hair.

They then had a great idea
to add a touch of class …
they made their Mum some orange juice
served in a champagne glass.

Wanting it to be just right
for Mum on her special day,
they picked the neighbour's roses
to decorate the tray.

Creeping upstairs to her bedroom,
the kids burst through the door …
'It's Mother's Day!' they both yelled,
as the toast fell on the floor.

They climbed under the covers,
tickling her with cold toes,
opened all of her presents
and shoved the soap under her nose.

Mum ate all of her breakfast,
saying that it was yummy.
The kids thought that, next year, they'd
make more to fill her tummy.

Caught up in the excitement,
puppy chased his tail around,
eating some bits of toast
and lumpy pancake that he'd found.

Mum loved every present
and said thank-you to everyone.
The kids and Dad looked on with pride
as she was having so much fun.

While Mum cleaned up the kitchen,
the others went out to play.
Dad and the kids all agreed
they'd had the greatest Mother's Day!